A TREE
FULL OF
MITZVOS

DINA HERMAN ROSENFELD

illustrated by

YOEL KENNY

Copyright © 1985
2ND PRTG. 1990
Merkos L'inyonei Chinuch, Inc.
770 Eastern Parkway, Brooklyn, N.Y. 11213
(718) 774-4000   493-9250

ISBN 0-8266-0418-8
Library of Congress Catalog Card Number 84-82261
Manufactured in the United States of America

Once upon a time, there was a little maple tree that lived very close to a big red house.

The little tree was very happy growing there, because he could see the family inside and all the things they did.

He watched them work,

and rest,

and eat,

and play.

But the most special treat of all, what the little tree loved most, was to see the family doing mitzvos.

In the morning, the little tree could see everyone saying Modeh Ani and Shema,

and giving tzedakah.

And, there was nothing the little tree liked better
than to see the family prepare for Shabbos!
When everything was ready, the little girl and

her mother would light the Shabbos candles, and
the little tree would bend over so he could hear
their bracha and say, "Amen."

Of course, at Chanukah time, the little tree had a wonderful view of the beautiful menorah, right in the window next to him.

Seeing all of these mitzvos made the little tree happy, but sometimes, he wished that *he* could do a mitzva, too!

"Oh," thought the little tree, "if only there was a mitzva for me!"

One day, just before Succos, the little tree thought that he'd found a mitzva to do. The whole family was busy building a succah outside on the grass.

"Maybe I can help," thought the little tree. "All of the other mitzvos are inside the house, but this one is right here near me!"

The little tree noticed that the family was piling cut branches on top of the succah for s'chach. "If I bend over," thought the tree, "I can be part of the succah, too!"

The little tree leaned over slowly and soon was touching the top of the succah! Never had he felt so very happy.

Suddenly, one of the boys said, "Look, father, the tree is touching our succah! I learned that for the succah roof you must only use branches *cut* from trees, and you must *not* build a succah under a tree!"

"Well," said Father, "let's straighten this tree and pull it back so it won't lean on our succah!"

The little tree felt himself being lifted back, away from the succah.

How disappointed he was!

The little tree was so unhappy that he began to cry.

"Oh," he said, "there are no mitzvos that trees can do — there are no mitzvos for me!"

"What's that you say?" said a little bird.

"I can't do any mitzvos," answered the tree.

"Oh, yes you can!" said the bird.

"If you let me build a nest in your branches, why, that's a big mitzva! Then my family will have a safe place to live."

"Mitzva? Who said mitzva?" asked a small squirrel.

"I want to do mitzvos," said the tree.

"Well, if you let me hide my acorns under your roots, that's a mitzva!

"When I'm hungry in the winter, I will have food to eat."

"I have a mitzva for you," said a vine growing on the ground.

"What is it?" asked the tree.

"If you let me grow around your trunk instead of staying here low on the ground, that's a mitzva, too! Then I will be high enough so that no one can step on me."

"Excuse me," whispered a yellow daisy, "but I know a mitzva."

"You do?" said the tree.

"Yes! If you let me grow in your shade, that's a mitzva! On hot summer days, my petals will stay fresh and cool and won't be burnt by the sun!"

"Helping others is a mitzva," said the bird.
"A very important one!" added the squirrel.
"We need your help!" pleaded the vine.
"Will you help us?" asked the daisy.

"Yes! Yes!" said the little tree, "I will help you all!

"Bird, you may build a nest in my branches.

"Squirrel, you may hide your acorns under my roots.

"Vine, you may grow around my trunk.

"Daisy, you may feel cool in my shade."

"Thank you!" chirped the bird.

"Thank you!" said the squirrel.

"Thank you! Thank you!" cried the vine.

"Thank you!" whispered the daisy.

"Thank all of you," said the little tree,

"for showing me some mitzvos that *I* can do!"

And the little tree was very happy, because he could do mitzvos at last.

GLOSSARY

BRACHA   blessing

CHANUKAH   Jewish Festival of Lights

MENORAH   candelabra usually for use on Chanukah

MITZVA   good deed, commandment from G-d

MITZVOS   plural of mitzva

S'CHACH   cut branches used for succah roof

SHABBOS   Sabbath

SUCCAH   a hut in which all meals are eaten during Succos

SUCCOS   Jewish Festival of Booths

TZEDAKAH   charity

OTHER TITLES IN THE
MERKOS YOUNG READERS' LIBRARY